For A.P.R. — a Klondike kid at heart.
JL

To Charlie and Jenny McTaggart.
KC

Text copyright © 2003 Julie Lawson
Illustrations copyright © 2003 Kasia Charko

National Library of Canada Cataloguing in Publication Data

Lawson, Julie, 1947 -

Arizona Charlie and the Klondike Kid / Julie Lawson ; [illustrations by] Kasia Charko.

ISBN 1-55143-250-1

1. Dawson (Yukon) — History — Juvenile literature. I. Charko, Kasia, 1949- II. Title.

PS8573.A933A94 2003   jC813'.54   C2002-911166-8

PZ7.L43828Ar 2003

First published in the United States, 2003

Library of Congress Control Number: 2002113060

Summary: In Dawson City in 1899, a boy longs to be a Wild West star just like Arizona Charlie.

Teacher's guide available from Orca Book Publishers.

Orca Book Publishers gratefully acknowledges the support of itspublishing programs provided by the following agencies: the Department of Canadian Heritage, the Canada Council for the Arts, and the British Columbia Arts Council.

Design by Christine Toller
Printed and bound in Hong Kong

IN CANADA:
Orca Book Publishers
1030 North Park Street
Victoria, BC Canada
V8T 1C6

IN THE UNITED STATES:
Orca Book Publishers
PO Box 468
Custer, WA   USA
98240-0468

05 04 03 • 5 4 3 2 1

Arizona Charlie AND THE KLONDIKE KID

WRITTEN BY JULIE LAWSON

ILLUSTRATED BY KASIA CHARKO

ORCA BOOK PUBLISHERS

ARIZONA CHARLIE WAS KING OF THE COWBOYS — a crack shot, a champion lasso twirler and a fearless horseman. He was famous all over the world. And he'd come to live in the gold rush town of Dawson City.

Soon after the champion's arrival, Ben saw him galloping through Dawson in pursuit of a runaway horse.

Whishhh! The lasso reached its target. Arizona Charlie reined in his horse, raised his sombrero and waved to the cheering crowd.

From that moment on, Ben longed to be a Wild West star — just like Arizona Charlie.

Every morning, Arizona Charlie practiced in an alley behind the Palace Grand Theater. Ben spied on him through a crack in the fence and copied every move.

Before long, he could twirl his lasso, jump in and out of the spinning loop and swirl it around his head.

He could lasso pieces of driftwood floating in the river.

He could lasso his friends — and on the run, too!

He set up tin cans and fired at them with his slingshot. Soon he could send them flying. From ten feet, then twenty feet — but no farther.

Not like Arizona Charlie. He could shoot the spots off a playing card at thirty feet.

One day, Ben was tearing into the alley, not watching where he was going, when he ran into something. *Ooff!* Down he went.

He caught his breath and looked up. Way up. Straight into the eyes of Arizona Charlie.

"You've been spying on me," the champion said. "I suppose you've got a good reason."

Ben gulped nervously. "I want to be a Wild West star," he said. "Just like you."

"You've got spunk," said Arizona Charlie. "I admire that." He stroked his mustache and eyed Ben thoughtfully. "How would you like to be in my show? I could use some help tomorrow night, in the closing act. Could you make it?"

"Could I?" Ben's face split in a grin. "Yes, sir!"

Ben could hardly contain his excitement.

He raced through town, telling everyone the news.

His family and friends were impressed.

"Arizona Charlie must've seen your tricks," Jack said. "Maybe he was spying on you."

"He must think you're awfully good," said Maggie.

Ben blushed with pride. "It just takes practice," he said.

All afternoon and into the night, Ben prepared for the show.

He practiced his twirls and jumps and spins.

He borrowed a scarf from his mother to wear around his neck.

He scrubbed his mud-stained hat and hung it out to dry.

He practiced bowing.

And as he lay in bed, unable to sleep, he thought about a new name. He needed something catchy. Something with a Wild West ring.

Dawson Ben? Yukon Benny? Ideas spun through his mind.

Then he had it. When he made his debut at the Palace Grand, he'd be known as the Klondike Kid.

The next night, Ben was seated in the theater, surrounded by family and friends. He took in the plush wallpaper, the gas lights, the balconies, the red velvet curtain — the Palace Grand certainly lived up to its name!

But Ben squirmed with impatience. When would the show begin? And how could he wait until the closing act?

Finally, the curtain rose. And there was Arizona Charlie, welcoming everyone to a night at the Palace Grand.

Soon Ben was caught up in the show. A band of outlaws, pursuing a cowboy. A display of bicycle riding. A juggling exhibition. A man on a flying trapeze.

Then the stage was awhirl with dancers, kicking up their heels to the rhythm of a ragtime tune. Everyone clapped in time to the music. Ben tapped his foot with renewed impatience.

At the end of the first act, his heart beat faster. The curtain came down. Before Ben knew it, Arizona Charlie was leading him onto the stage.

"Ten minutes till curtain," said Arizona Charlie. "Sit tight, kid. I'll be right back."

Sit tight? Impossible!

Ben twirled his lasso and bowed to the curtain. Before long, he'd be hearing howls of approval for the Klondike Kid.

He was finishing his fourth imaginary encore when Arizona Charlie returned, carrying three glass balls and a rifle.

Glass balls? A rifle? Ben hadn't figured on a sharp-shooting act.

"Don't look so worried!" Arizona Charlie handed Ben a glass ball. "It's a simple trick. You hold the ball, and I shoot it. My wife usually does it, but the other night a faulty bullet nicked the tip of her thumb."

Ben gripped his rope. "But my lasso! I thought — "

"'Course you can do your rope tricks! But that'll come later." He smiled at Ben and tipped his hat. "You'll do fine."

Ben looked at the glass ball. He looked at the rifle. He looked at his thumb.

On the other side of the curtain the audience was whooping it up, eager for the act to begin.

"Five seconds to curtain!"

Five, four, three, two —

The curtain began to rise.

Ben's heart thudded. His legs shook. His stomach lurched.

"Tonight we have a special guest," Arizona Charlie announced. "A young lad with a steady hand and more than a few rope tricks up his sleeve. I give you — the Klondike Kid!"

The applause was deafening.

Arizona Charlie strode across the stage and raised his rifle. "Hold the ball out to the left," he said. "I'll give you the count of three. One…Two…"

Ben swallowed hard. The lights, the noise, the staring eyes — he couldn't keep his hand steady. He could scarcely breathe. "I can't!" he stammered.

Arizona Charlie lowered his rifle, twirled his mustache and faced the audience. "Looks like the sharp-shooting act's on hold," he said. "So we'll move on to the lasso tricks. Once again, I give you — " He never finished.

Ben dropped the glass ball and grabbed his lasso. Then he tore off the stage, opened the side door and bolted into the street.

Crushed and humiliated, Ben slumped away from the Palace Grand. His eyes prickled with tears. He'd lost his chance. Now he'd never be the world-famous Klondike Kid.

Behind him, he could hear the crowd coming out of the theater. The show was over. He quickened his step, anxious that no one should see him. He was halfway down the street when a cry rang out.

"Stop, thief!"

A man burst through the crowd, pursued by an angry prospector.

"Stop!" The prospector had almost caught up when a pack of dogs sent him sprawling.

The thief kept running. So did the dogs. A team of mules added to the confusion.

When Ben saw that the thief was about to escape down an alley, he raised his lasso.

No stage fright now! Only the satisfying feel of the rope in his hands. Over his shoulders and over his head, the rope sailed through the air and *oooofff!* The thief fell to the ground.

A crowd gathered and a constable arrived on the scene. "Well done, son," he said.

The King of the Cowboys strode straight through the crowd and shook Ben's hand.

"I didn't mean to scare you back there," he said. "You've got spunk for more important things than a sharp-shooting act." He turned and faced the crowd. "Come on, everybody. Hats off — to the Klondike Kid!"

"Hip hip hooray!" they cheered.

Ben gave a modest bow. And blushed to the tips of his ears.

Charlie Meadows, known as Arizona Charlie, came to Dawson City, Yukon, during the Klondike Gold Rush in 1897. On his arrival, he published an illustrated journal called the *Klondike News* and set to work building the Palace Grand Theater. The theater opened on July 18, 1899, and was described as "the best Vaudeville house west of Chicago."

 One of the most popular acts was a shooting exhibition in which Arizona Charlie would shoot glass balls held by his wife. One night he missed and nicked her thumb, bringing an end to the sharp-shooting act.

 In 1901, Arizona Charlie sold the Palace Grand and left Dawson City. To this day, however, every summer thousands of visitors and Dawson residents attend the colorful shows at the reconstructed Palace Grand Theater where the spirit of Arizona Charlie lives on.